This book belongs to

_____

With love to Margot, Amy and Sophie.
— Libby

For my big sisters.
— Jedda

First American Edition 2021
Kane Miller, A Division of EDC Publishing

Text copyright © Libby Gleeson 2020
Illustrations copyright © Jedda Robaard 2020

First published in 2020 in Australia by Little Hare Books,
an imprint of Hardie Grant Egmont.

For information contact:
Kane Miller, A Division of EDC Publishing
P.O. Box 470663,
Tulsa, OK 74147-0663
www.kanemiller.com
www.usbornebooksandmore.com
www.edcpub.com

Library of Congress Control Number: 2020936862

Printed in Shenzhen, Guangdong Province, China
ISBN: 978-1-68464-211-3
1 2 3 4 5 6 7 8 9 10

Soon

Libby Gleeson Jedda Robaard

Kane Miller
A DIVISION OF EDC PUBLISHING

We're waiting for our baby.

Wait, wait, wait.

"When will the baby come, Mom?"

"Soon."

We wash the tiny clothes.
Wash, wash, wash.
Splash, splash, splash.
"When will the baby come, Mom?"

"Soon."

We paint the baby's crib.
Paint, paint, paint.
Splatter, splatter, splatter.

"When will the baby
come, Mom?"

"Soon."

We sort all the toys.

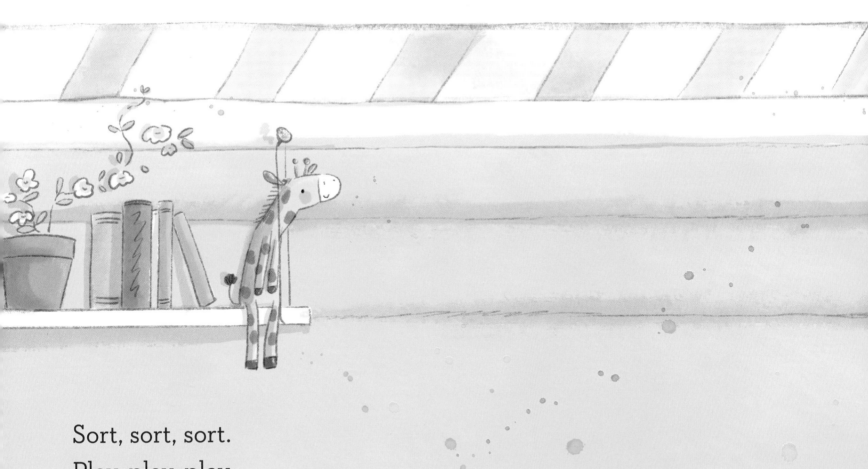

Sort, sort, sort.
Play, play, play.
"When will the baby come, Mom?"

"Soon."

Our baby must be nearly here.

"Will it be today, Mom?"

Mom shakes her head.
"Soon," is all she says.

I pat Mom's tummy.

Pat, pat, pat.

Our baby bumps my hand.
Bump, bump, bump.

"Will the baby ever come, Mom?"

"I think so. I know so."
Mom sighs.
Sigh, sigh, sigh.

And we wait a bit longer.

Wait, wait, wait.

And then, and
then, and then ...